DISNEY'S
CLIMB ABOARD IF YOU DARE!

STORIES FROM THE PIRATES OF THE CARIBBEAN

BY NICHOLAS STEPHENS
ILLUSTRATED BY ROBERTA COLLIER-MORALES

DISNEY PRESS

NEW YORK

Printed in the United States of America.

First Edition

1 3 5 7 9 10 8 6 4 2

Library of Congress Catalog Number: 96-83600

ISBN 0-7868-4061-7 (pbk.)
ISBN 0-7868-5033-7 (lib. bdg.)

CONTENTS

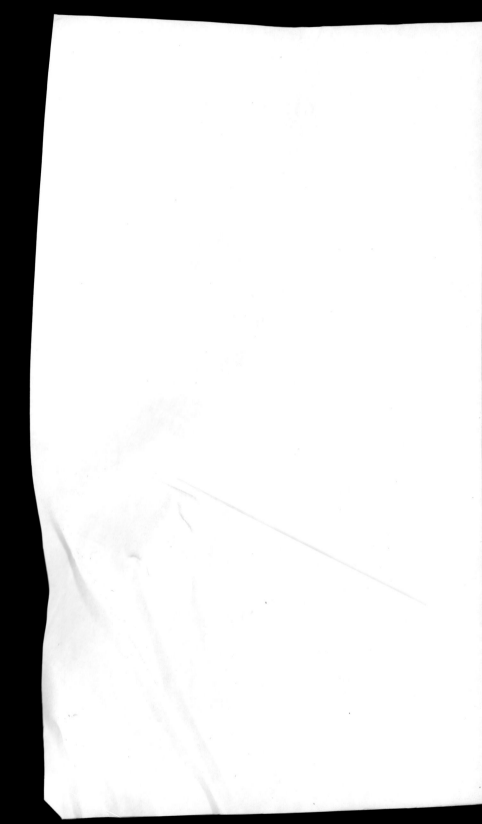

BUCCANEERS, READERS, AND OTHER SCALAWAGS TAKE HEED!

Here follows the true tale of *Buzzard's* Bounty, a treasure so vast that one glance at its riches turned good men into scoundrels . . . and scoundrels into pirates.

It all begins with Sharkheart Sam, the cunningest rogue on the Caribbean (and some say the nastiest, too). In his lightning-quick sloop, the *Buzzard*, Sharkheart amassed a huge fortune, plundering all who crossed his path. For many long years he terrorized the high seas, until he met his end at the hands of a lad not much older than you.

That brave lad escaped from Sharkheart's clutches with a chest of precious jewels, but the rest of the treasure still remains to be discovered. Did it wash up on a remote desert isle? Or is it still lying at the bottom of the deep blue sea?

Should you dare to go searching for the treasure, keep a lookout for unsavory types with a gleam in their eye and a parrot on their shoulder. Rumor has it that the treasure is guarded day and night by the ghost of Sharkheart Sam himself, a greedy buzzard to the very end.

Account Book of the BUZZARD

93 Bags Gold Dust
11 Silver Candlesticks
132 Fine Ladies' Rings
12 Emerald Necklaces
22 Gold Lockets
11 Large Bags Silver Bars (935 ounces)
6 Large Bags Coined Gold (342 ounces)
8 Bags Containing Pieces of Eight and New
   English Crowns
18 Rubies, Small and Great
7 Handkerchiefs of Gold Dust (149 ounces)
1 Bag Unpolished Stones (74 ounces)
1 Bag Silver Buttons (29 ounces)
101 Bales of Merchandise, Including Calico,
   Muslins, Canvas, Silk, and Bags of Sugar
1 Iron Box, Filled to the Brim with Precious
   Stones

THE SINKING OF
SHARKHEART SAM

"Halt, you miserable little street pirate!"

Pablo didn't wait to see who was after him. The clatter of swords told him all he needed to know. The king's guards were on his trail. Three of them this time.

He dashed through narrow cobblestone alleys toward the docks, tightly clutching the gold coins he'd stolen out of a gentleman's pocket.

Pablo didn't like having to pick pockets. But he was an orphan, and a boy had to eat after all. And he was a pickpocket of principle—he stole only from those who would still dine well when the day was done.

At the top of the hill, the port came into view. Pablo gasped at the ship anchored near the docks.

It was big as a city, a square-rigger with more cannons than he could count.

A large group of men was gathered at the docks. Pablo dashed down the hill and dived into the crowd.

"Hey, matey, no need to shove," a young man complained.

Pablo crouched low. "Pardon, sir," he said breathlessly.

"No 'sir' for me. I go by the name of Turi." The young man grinned. He was tall and slender, with wide, dark eyes.

Pablo peeked over his shoulder for signs of the guards. "What are you all waiting for?" he asked.

"We're signing on to serve on the *Santa Catalina*," Turi answered. "The king's finest galleon, she is! Heading for Zaragona with supplies and weapons."

"What's Zaragona?" Pablo asked.

"It's the king's biggest colony in the Caribbean," Turi said. "The colonists there are in desperate need of aid. It's a dangerous mission, with those cutthroats ruling the waters."

"Cutthroats?"

"Sharkheart Sam and his men. The bloodiest pirate on the high seas. He's waylaid the last two missions to Zaragona."

Behind him, shouts rang out. Pablo turned to see the three guards at the top of the hill. "We'll get you yet, you little devil!" one yelled.

"There's some fellows I wouldn't want for friends," Turi said, winking at Pablo.

Pablo crouched even lower. "Two more men for this load," announced a lieutenant dressed in a fancy coat and breeches. He pointed to a longboat filled with new recruits.

"Looks like I'm next," Turi said. "See you on board."

Pablo swallowed past the lump in his throat. The guards were searching along the edge of the crowd. He was done for, unless . . .

As Turi finished signing up, Pablo stepped forward boldly. "And just how old might *you* be?" the lieutenant sneered.

"Old enough to serve His Majesty with honor," Pablo said.

"Step aside. You're too young, and too skinny to boot."

Pablo sighed. It was true that he was small and thin for his age. He glanced back at the guards, then out at the big ship rolling slowly on the vast ocean. Which would it be? Prison or pirates? It was not a happy choice.

Pablo slipped the lieutenant one of his precious gold coins. "I'd be much obliged if you'd reconsider, sir."

The lieutenant fingered the shiny coin. "Come to think of it, you're not too skinny to swab the decks." He handed Pablo a ledger. "Sign your name, lad."

Pablo had just finished writing when he heard a loud cry.

"There he is, the little sewer rat!"

In a flash, Pablo leapt into the longboat. "Cast off men!" the lieutenant ordered.

The oarsmen began to row. The longboat slipped away just as the guards reached the edge of the dock.

"Let him go, and good riddance," one of the guards said loudly. "He'll never survive the trip anyway. If the storms don't get him, the pirates surely will!"

✕

For what had to be the hundredth time in a week, Pablo leaned over the side of the *Santa Catalina*. He'd been seasick so many times he'd lost track.

"At least you're not pea green anymore," Turi commented as he scoured the deck with a soft piece of sandstone. "Today you're more of a fish-belly white, I'd say. Very becoming."

"They tell me I should have my sea legs by now. But I don't even have my sea feet," Pablo said with a sigh.

Just then, Zita, the baby orangutan who lived on board the ship, leaped down from the rigging onto Pablo's shoulder. Although Zita belonged to the captain, she'd somehow decided that Pablo was her true owner.

"She certainly has taken a liking to you," Turi said.

"You have to watch her carefully. She'll steal anything. Yesterday she took my salt pork when I wasn't looking," complained Pablo.

"Birds of a feather," Turi said with a laugh.

Pablo gave Zita an affectionate scratch on the ear. He'd never had a pet before, unless you counted the street cats that sometimes slept with him on cold nights.

Turi gazed out to sea, shading his eyes with his hand. "What's that off the starboard bow?"

"No doubt another seabird you've decided is the *Buzzard*," Pablo teased. The *Buzzard* was Sharkheart Sam's ship, the fastest pirate ship on the high seas.

"I've heard rumors that our hold is filled to the brim with gold for the viceroy of Zaragona," Turi said. "Can you doubt for a moment that Sharkheart will try to capture it?"

"First he'd have to *know* about it, Turi."

"Pirates can smell gold from a thousand miles off," Turi said, "and he's the greediest, meanest pirate on the seas." He lowered his voice. "A gunner's mate told me that Sharkheart once cut off a sailor's ear and forced him to eat it with a knife and fork and a dash of pepper."

"No salt?" Pablo joked.

"You laugh now," Turi said, "but we'll see how brave you are when the cannons are blasting."

"Pirates don't scare me. Why, I'm a bit of a street

pirate myself. I'm so fast I could pick the captain's pocket in front of the whole crew, and no one would be the wiser."

Turi rolled his eyes. "If I had a gold coin for every time you bragged, I'd be richer than Sharkheart himself!"

Pablo smiled. "Maybe I'll just *show* you how good a pirate I am."

✕

That night, the sea was calm and the moon was hidden behind a thick blanket of clouds. Pablo woke Turi, who was snoring loudly in his swinging hammock. Quietly they sneaked up to the quarter-deck, slipping past the watch sentries.

"Where are we going?" Turi asked in a nervous whisper.

"The captain's quarters," Pablo answered. "Inside his sea chest is a silver teapot as shiny as a new moon."

"And *how* exactly do you know this?"

"I sneaked inside once. Just to look things over."

Turi stopped dead in his tracks. "Are you out of your mind? Do you know what they do to thieves, Pablo? Do you know what they do to thieves who steal from the *captain*? They make them run the gauntlet! The crew forms two lines, and the thief walks between them while they whip him!"

"That's only if they catch him, Turi. And I don't intend to get caught," Pablo said with a confident grin. "Besides, I'm not going to *steal* the teapot. I'm just going to borrow it, to show you what a cunning pirate I can be."

"Don't be a fool!"

Don't worry. I won't get caught. You just wait here," Pablo instructed.

Near the door to the captain's cabin, a guard was snoozing.

Pablo knew he would have to be extra stealthy to get past the dozing guard. Complete quiet was the key. You had to move fast, but not too fast—

Umphh!

Two long arms grabbed Pablo from behind! A sentry had discovered him, and was going to choke him till he—

Pablo took hold of the arms. They were hairy.

Very hairy.

"Zita!" he whispered. "I told you to stay below-decks!"

Zita responded by slipping her paw into Pablo's pocket to steal one of his gold coins. "Stop, you fuzzy little thief," Pablo said. "We've got better things to take."

With Zita riding on his back, Pablo stepped over the guard and eased open the cabin door. The captain was sleeping soundly, his mouth wide open as he snored. Pablo tiptoed to the chest at the foot of the captain's hanging cot. Without making a sound, he scooped out the silver teapot.

But Zita wasn't interested in silver. She reached into Pablo's pocket and pulled out a gold coin triumphantly.

"Zita!" Pablo cried in a loud whisper. He grabbed for the coin, but Zita gleefully tossed it across the room. To Pablo's horror, it landed right in the captain's open mouth.

He jerked up, eyes wide, and spat out the coin. "What in the devil—"

"Begging your pardon, sir," Pablo said, the teapot in his hand. "Would this be a bad time for some polishing?"

"You'll face the gauntlet for this, thief. And for good measure, I may toss that stupid ape over the side!"

✕

"If only you'd listened to me," Turi said sadly the next day.

Pablo gazed down the long line of seamen, each holding a piece of rope. He would be lucky to come out of this alive. Well, it was his own fault for bragging about being such a cunning pirate. He was a miserable thief, and nothing more. A poor orphan who would never amount to anything. He deserved whatever punishment he got.

Mr. Rodriguez, the first lieutenant, stood in front of him, his cutlass poised. "This," he said, pointing to the sharp blade, "is to keep you from running too fast as you're whipped. I'll walk in front of you as

you head down the line. Thieves tend to be cowards, you know."

The captain joined them. "I'm in a merciful frame of mind today, so I've decided to spare the life of that wretched ape," he said. "Instead I've had her imprisoned."

One of the carpenter's mates appeared, carrying a small wooden cage. Zita sat inside, looking miserable.

The captain turned to Mr. Rodriguez. "Commence the gauntlet."

"Aye, sir." Mr. Rodriguez raised his cutlass high. "At my signal, men."

Pablo took a deep breath. Just as Mr. Rodriguez lowered his cutlass, Turi's cry rang out.

"Ship off the larboard bow!" he cried. "*Pirate ship!*"

"Mr. Rodriguez," the captain snapped, "my spyglass." The captain gazed through his brass telescope. "It's the *Buzzard*," he confirmed grimly. "We've got our work cut out for us now. A big galleon like ours will never outmaneuver her. She's too fast."

"Your orders, Captain?" asked Mr. Rodriguez.

"Clear for battle. Run out the cannons!" the captain said. "We'll give them a taste of iron and see how they like it. I won't give up the king's gold without a fight!"

"All hands!" Mr. Rodriguez cried. "Clear for battle!"

Instantly the crew went into action. Sharpshooters climbed into the rigging with their muskets. Seamen called "powder monkeys" ran to retrieve cartridges of gunpowder. Other seamen spread damp sand along the decks to keep the crew from slipping as they rushed—and to soak up any blood. Meanwhile, most of the crew labored to ready the heavy cannons.

The captain looked at Pablo and shook his head. "Looks like one pirate's spared another," he said. "There'll be time enough for you later. For now, make yourself useful."

Turi rushed to Pablo's side. He was trembling.

Sharkheart's ship was closing fast, bearing down on the *Santa Catalina* like a huge vulture. "You're saved, for a while at least," Turi said. He gazed at the swiftly moving pirate ship, his face white. "But what if they take us prisoner, Pablo? I don't want to eat my ears! I like my ears! I *need* my ears!"

"Relax, Turi," Pablo said, but his own voice was quavering. "We've got powder to fetch for the cannons. But first, I've a prisoner to release."

Pablo ran to Zita's cage and opened it. The little monkey flew into his arms. "Down belowdecks for you, Zita," Pablo said, pulling free. "You'll be no good to us when the cannonballs start flying."

But Zita was in no mood to miss the action. She clambered up the foremast, chattering away happily.

By the time Pablo and Turi returned from the chamber where the gunpowder was stored, Sharkheart's sloop was so close that Pablo could hear the pirates' taunts.

"Fire a broadside, men," the captain ordered.

BOOM! Three dozen cannons went off at once. The entire ship vibrated. Smoke filled the air.

"Reload and fire at will!" the captain cried.

Pablo passed a cartridge of gunpowder to one of the gunners. Just then the entire world seemed to explode. The pirates were firing back! Huge cannonballs zipped by, just inches from Pablo's head.

C-R-R-A-C-K!

"The foremast!" a gunner cried. "It's been hit!"

Pablo watched in horror as the huge mast fell slowly, like a great oak. "Zita!" he screamed. The orangutan clung to the mast for dear life.

The mast hit the water with a huge splash. The pirates on the *Buzzard* cheered and applauded. Dodging cannons and crew, Pablo ran to the bow, with Turi following close behind.

The mast submerged, then resurfaced. Zita was hanging on to the end of the mast, tangled in wet sails and rope. Her little head was barely visible as she rode the waves.

"I've got to save her," Pablo said.

"Pablo, no!" Turi cried. "There are sharks in those waters, not to mention cannonballs!"

But Pablo was already climbing over the side. He took a great swan dive, flying through the air for what seemed like an eternity while cannonballs whizzed past.

When he came up for air, Pablo saw Zita fifty yards away. He was not a strong swimmer, and by the time he reached the mast his arms and legs were burning. Just as he grabbed hold of the slick wood, a cannonball landed a few feet away, throwing up a huge curtain of water.

When the waves had subsided, Zita clambered nimbly along the mast to meet Pablo. She jumped on to his back, hanging on to his neck so tightly he could barely swallow.

A shout from the *Buzzard* caught Pablo's attention. Two pirates had noticed Pablo and Zita. They aimed their muskets straight at Pablo. He slipped underwater, holding tight to Zita with one hand and to the broken mast with the other.

Even submerged, he could hear the sharp *zing* of the musketballs as they hit the water. When he couldn't hold his breath any longer, Pablo went up for air. Zita, furious and sputtering, yanked on his hair to show her annoyance.

Just then the *Santa Catalina* let go another broadside. But Sharkheart was moving too fast. All the cannonballs missed their mark.

Bobbing next to the mast, Pablo watched in frustration as the battle raged. The captain had been right. No matter how he tried to angle for position, the *Buzzard* would always be swifter. And in a battle like this, position was everything.

Another of the *Buzzard*'s volleys hit its mark, carving a hole in the *Santa Catalina*'s hull. Pablo knew the ship's carpenters would rush to repair the damage. This time, it wasn't enough to sink her. Good thing it hadn't hit the handling chamber where the gunpowder was stored. That would have been the end of her . . .

Suddenly Pablo had a dangerous idea. It was crazy. It was probably suicidal. But what did he have to lose?

The *Buzzard* was coming around. In a few seconds, she would go sailing right past Pablo. "Get ready, Zita!"

The pirate ship seemed impossibly tall as it raced past. Pablo knew he had to be quick. A rope was dangling over the side. It was part of the rigging, shot away during the battle.

In an instant, he snatched the rope and pulled himself up, up and over the side, onto the deck of the *Buzzard*.

The entire pirate crew was on the other side of the ship, firing cannons that faced the *Santa Catalina*.

Wet and scared, Pablo crouched behind a large barrel. He could jut make out an imposing figure barking orders. He was tall and broad shouldered, with a red silk sash around his waist. His silver cutlass gleamed in the sun. Across his cheek was a deep, ugly scar. Every finger on his hand glittered with jewels.

"Sharkheart Sam," Pablo whispered. "What I'd give for just one of those jewels, Zita!"

Without another thought, Pablo slipped down a hatch belowdecks in search of Sharkheart's cabin. If he could steal a teapot out of his own captain's quarters, why not a diamond or two out of Sharkheart Sam's?

Pablo came to a lavishly appointed cabin that clearly belonged to Sharkheart. On a desk he found an account book for the *Buzzard*. He scanned the most recent entry and gasped. He couldn't read very well, but he knew enough to understand the list. Gold dust! Silver bars! Candlesticks!

And then there was the last item on the list, the most tantalizing of all: 1 IRON BOX, FILLED TO THE BRIM WITH PRECIOUS STONES.

Pablo searched high and low while the cannons boomed outside. He had to get his hands on that iron box!

But try as he may, he could not find a trace of Sharkheart's vast treasure.

"Well, Zita," he said at last, "we can't risk looking any longer. I'd better get on with my plan."

As he eased open the door to see if it was safe to leave, Zita leapt onto Sharkheart's swinging cot. "This is not a good time to play, Zita," Pablo scolded.

Zita grabbed one of Sharkheart's feather pillows and ran back to Pablo. "Come on, Zita," he urged, but she refused to let go of the pillow.

Pablo grabbed it away. "Come *on*, I said—" He stopped cold. The pillow was heavy.

Heavy and hard.

Frantically, Pablo ripped open the pillow. Feathers went flying as he dug deep into its center. At last he retrieved a square iron box. He opened it slowly, fingers trembling.

"Diamonds!" he whispered. "Rubies! And . . . what are those green ones called? Zita, you are now the richest orangutan in the Caribbean. In the world, I'd venture!"

Zita grabbed a handful of diamonds, chattering happily.

"We'll count them later," Pablo said. "First, we have work to do!"

He grabbed a lantern and lit it, then tucked the treasure chest under his shirt.

With Zita in tow, Pablo made his way to the handling chamber. A gunner was making up powder cartridges for the cannons. His back was turned.

Pablo set the lantern by the door and slipped in. Now came the hard part. Using his best pickpocket technique, he tiptoed over and grabbed a small keg of powder. He opened it and poured a trail of powder leading away from the kegs.

One step at a time, Pablo eased toward the door, keeping a steady eye on the gunner, who was still busily making cartridges. Just a few more steps and then—

"Going somewhere?"

Pablo spun around. Sharkheart Sam himself stood before him!

"I believe you have something of mine," Sharkheart said. "One of my men saw you leaving my cabin and called me." He grinned. "You're a spunky lad." Then his smile evaporated. "As it happens, I hate spunky lads."

Sharkheart held out his hand. "My treasure, boy."

Pablo glanced at the lantern near his feet. One spark, and the trail of powder would ignite, blowing the entire ship to pieces in a matter of moments. But how could he get off the ship in time?

"The treasure, before I cut off your ears!"

Pablo gulped.

"My jewels, now!" Sharkheart screamed. He grabbed for Pablo.

Suddenly Zita leapt through the air. She landed on Sharkheart's arm and bit down with her very sharp teeth.

"*Yowwwww!*" the pirate captain squealed.

"Let's go, Zita!" Pablo shouted. Zita jumped back

onto Pablo's shoulder. Pablo flung the lantern at the trail of gunpowder and ran like he had never run before.

Down the companionway! Up the ladder! Out of the hatch!

He raced to the rail and leapt out over the water just as the fire belowdecks reached the end of the gunpowder trail.

BA-BOOOOM!

Pablo hit the water and went under. By the time he came back up, the *Buzzard* was just a smoking wreck. The captain and crew of the *Santa Catalina*, upon hearing how much bounty was in the *Buzzard*, considered trying to rescue it—for the king, of course. A few daring crewmen made dives to retrieve the treasure but it had scattered when the ship was blown to pieces, and the most they could get was a few bags of gold and some silver candlesticks. Pablo had managed to keep his box of precious gems.

X

When they reached Marito, the main port city of Zaragona, with all of the gold from the king and the addition of Sharkheart Sam's treasure, a great celebration was held in Pablo's honor. The viceroy, who had no children of his own, was so impressed with Pablo's courage that he decided to make Pablo his heir. Pablo would someday take over as viceroy himself. His box of jewels and the rest of the

treasure became known as *Buzzard*'s Bounty.

Never again did Pablo have to pick pockets. Even Zita lost her taste for stealing, after the viceroy had a jewel necklace made just for her.

It was beautiful to behold, gold encrusted with rubies and diamonds . . . and those green things, too.

A PIRATE'S LIFE
FOR ME

The first thing Carmelita noticed was the parrot. She'd seen green parrots and red parrots and yellow parrots, and even green-and-red-and-yellow parrots, but she'd never, ever seen a parrot with a little black patch over his eye.

It was perched on the shoulder of a most unsavory-looking gentleman. As he swaggered into the inn Carmelita's parents owned, the smell of rum filled the air. He was wearing a tricorne hat with a bright yellow feather. A shiny gold earring hung from his ear, and a cutlass hung from his side. His wooden leg clumped on the floor as he approached. Covering his right eye was a black eye patch, just like his parrot's.

"Mark my words, that's a pirate, sure as can be,"

Carmelita whispered to her mother.

"If he's got gold to spend on a room, he'll be welcome here," her mother said. "Understand?"

"But Mama," Carmelita pressed, "the earring and the parrot and the patch and the wooden leg . . . He *must* be a pirate!"

The man paused to set down his trunk. "Welcome, sir," said Carmelita's father. "What can we do for you?"

"A room for the week," the man said gruffly. He slammed down three gold coins on the counter. "I'll need my privacy, you understand, and plenty of rum."

"Plenty of rum! Plenty of rum for Mr. Bleek!" the parrot squawked.

"Shut up, you miserable feather duster," the man grumbled.

"What's your parrot's name, Mr. Bleek?" Carmelita asked.

"Goes by the name of Bartholomew," he answered.

"What happened to his eye?"

"He asked too many questions, that's what happened," Mr. Bleek said with a menacing glare.

"Please forgive her," said Carmelita's father. "She's a very curious child." He handed Mr. Bleek a key. "First room on the right upstairs. We'll see that you're not disturbed."

Carmelita watched Mr. Bleek slowly climb the

stairs. His wooden leg made a steady *thump, thump, thump.* "*Now* will you admit he's a pirate?" she whispered to her parents.

"Nonsense. He's just colorful," her mother said, although she didn't sound entirely convinced.

"Remember that time you were sure one of our guests was the viceroy of Zaragona himself?" her father pointed out.

Carmelita frowned. "Well, he *did* have clothes made of real silk. And a ruby ring as big as my fist."

"You leave Mr. Bleek be," her father advised. "Whatever his business, it's no business of ours."

With a sigh, Carmelita headed upstairs to make beds. As she passed Mr. Bleek's room, she heard an odd noise behind the door. Someone was singing in a high-pitched, nasal voice.

She pressed her ear to the door. It was Bartholomew!

"Yo-ho, yo-ho," he sang, "a pirate's life for me!"

So Mr. Bleek *was* a pirate! But why was he here in Zaragona?

Suddenly the door flew open. Mr. Bleek stood before her, wild-eyed, his cutlass raised. "What in blazes are you doing here?" he boomed.

"Pardon, sir," Carmelita said in a squeaky voice. "I was just wondering if you'd be wanting some fresh linens."

Mr. Bleek grabbed her arm so tightly it burned. "Listen, my girl, I want just one thing, and that's to be left alone! Next time, you might not be so lucky with this blade. Understand?"

"I . . . I understand," Carmelita said, backing away.

As she dashed down the hall, trembling, she could still hear Bartholomew singing away happily, "Yo-ho, yo-ho, a pirate's life for me!"

✕

When Mr. Bleek left the inn early the next morning, Carmelita decided to follow him. Hiding behind bushes and sneaking down alleyways, she shadowed him up and down the streets of Marito. Once she thought she saw Bartholomew peering back at her with his one good eye, but she couldn't be sure.

Mr. Bleek made his way past the busy docks until he came to a quiet stretch of coastline. He sat in the shade of some palm trees and pulled out a piece of paper from his vest pocket. Studying the sandy coast with great care, he began to sketch.

Crouching low in the sea grass, Carmelita waited patiently until Mr. Bleek finally dozed off. When she was sure he was asleep, she shinnied up a palm tree just a few yards from the spot where Mr. Bleek was snoring away. Hidden in the uppermost fronds, Carmelita could plainly see the piece of paper he was working on.

It was a map! He was making a map of the port and the nearby coastline. Carmelita was sure she

knew why. Mr. Bleek and his pirate friends were preparing to invade Zaragona!

But who would believe her? Her parents would say she was imagining things. And if she went to the viceroy's guards and told them . . . Well, she could hear their laughter even now.

No, she would have to find a way to deal with this herself.

Perhaps she was just a young girl with a big imagination, but Carmelita Lopez was determined to save Zaragona from the wily Mr. Bleek and his fellow buccaneers.

Now all she had to do was figure out how.

✕

Her hands shaking, Carmelita knocked on Mr. Bleek's door. She was carrying the bottle of rum her father had given her. It was the third one she'd offered to deliver to Mr. Bleek that evening.

"Mr. Bleek, sir? I've brought more rum for you."

He didn't answer. Her heart icy with fear, Carmelita eased open the door, on alert for any sign of Mr. Bleek's sharp cutlass. But he was nowhere to be seen.

Bartholomew sat perched on the windowsill. "The pirate is pickled!" he announced.

Carmelita tiptoed into the room. There, on the other side of the bed, lay Mr. Bleek. He was passed out cold.

"Well, well," she murmured, "I'm in luck."

Quickly she checked his coat pocket for the map. Nothing. She tried under the mattress, under his pillow, in his sea chest. No map. She tried every last corner of the room. At last she sank down on the bed, discouraged.

"The pirate is pickled!" Bartholomew cried. "The pickle is pirated!"

"Sounds like you're a little pickled yourself," Carmelita said.

Bartholomew cocked his head, blinking his shiny black eye.

Carmelita sighed. What could he have done with the map? She didn't have much time. Mr. Bleek could wake up at any moment.

"Where would someone hide a map?" she muttered.

"Wooden leg!"

Carmelita gasped. "What did you say, Bartholomew?"

"Wooden leg!" the parrot squawked. "Wooden leg!"

Carmelita knelt beside Mr. Bleek. The leg seemed to be made of two pieces that screwed together. If one piece was hollow inside, it would be the perfect place to hide a map. Well, it was worth a try . . . unless, of course, she woke up the pirate. One glance at his razor-sharp cutlass told her she didn't want to be around for *that*.

Taking a deep breath, Carmelita ever so gently tried to unscrew the leg. It wouldn't budge. She tried again. Mr. Bleek grunted like a wild hog.

She tried again with all her might, and this time the bottom section of the leg slowly came unscrewed. Sure enough, inside was the rolled-up map Mr. Bleek had drawn that day. At the bottom of the map was scrawled a note: MIDNIGHT, THE EIGHTH—RENDEZVOUS WITH THE *SEA DEMON* ONE MILE NORTH OF PORT.

The *Sea Demon*! Carmelita had heard her parents speak of that ship, a notorious pirate vessel that had captured and destroyed some of the king's best frigates. And Mr. Bleek planned to meet it tonight!

Quickly Carmelita screwed the leg back together. "Bartholomew," she said, stroking the parrot's soft feathers, "I don't know how to thank you. If I'm successful, I promise I'll save you from Mr. Bleek and care for you all your days."

If she survived. It was a big if.

✕

For the next hour, Carmelita sat in her room, redrawing Mr. Bleek's map by candlelight. She was careful to change the details so that a pirate aiming for the port would end up instead on the rocky and treacherous coastline to the south.

When she was done, she tiptoed down the hall to the pirate's room. Carmelita knocked softly on Mr. Bleek's door. He didn't answer. She was not surprised. With any luck at all, he'd sleep for hours.

Carmelita slipped into the room. She knelt beside the pirate and unscrewed his leg while Bartholomew watched silently.

Suddenly, just as she slipped her new map into the hollow bottom leg, Mr. Bleek awoke with a start! Carmelita leapt back in horror.

Black eyes burning, the pirate grabbed for his cutlass. "I should have slit your little throat while I had the chance!" he bellowed. "You think you can outsmart Mr. Bleek, you nosy child? You know what they say about curiosity and the cat?"

Carmelita gulped.

"Killed it!" Bartholomew cried gleefully. "Killed the kitty!"

"Shut up, you feather brain!" Mr. Bleek screeched. He grabbed an empty rum bottle and flung it at Bartholomew. The parrot flapped out of its path, just in the nick of time. The bottle hit the

wall and shattered into a thousand pieces.

"And now for you!" Mr. Bleek cried. He started to struggle to his feet, but with only half his wooden leg it was difficult to stand. With a furious groan, he stumbled onto his knees.

"Aargh!" he screamed.

He grabbed for the bottom part of the leg. So did Carmelita. Mr. Bleek had one end. She had the other.

He yanked. She yanked. "Give me my leg, you little brat!" he screeched.

Carmelita tried desperately to hang on, but her fingers were slipping on the shiny wood.

"I'll slice you into bits and feed you to the fish!" Mr. Bleek cried.

Suddenly a flutter of wings filled the air. Bartholomew swooped over. He landed right on Mr. Bleek's head, clutching with sharp claws. Instantly the pirate let go of the leg.

"Unhand me, pigeon breath, or I'll turn you into a ladies' hat!" Mr. Bleek shouted.

Carmelita knew what she had to do. She lifted the heavy leg high over her head. "Look out, Bartholomew!" she yelled.

WHAM! She walloped the pirate on his head, just as the parrot dodged aside.

"Ouch," Mr. Bleek groaned. He fell to the ground with an enormous thud.

"Ouch," Bartholomew repeated, primly rearranging his feathers.

Carmelita pulled her carefully redrawn map out of the leg. "Now what?" she moaned. Her wonderful plan was in ruins.

"Yo-ho, yo-ho," Bartholomew sang, "a pirate's life for me."

"It'll be a pirate's life for all of us unless I can come up with another idea," Carmelita said. "And I don't think I'd look very good in pirates' garb."

She paused as a daring idea began to take hold. "Then again," she said to Bartholomew, "I *might* look rather dashing in an eye patch."

✕

At five minutes to midnight, Carmelita found herself pacing the edge of the shore with a parrot perched on her shoulder. One mile north of town, Mr. Bleek's note had said, but there were numerous landing places where a small boat might come to shore. She had picked the most protected spot. It wasn't the easiest place to land a boat, but it seemed like the kind of location a pirate would choose.

Carmelita wasn't just hoping to think like a pirate. She was hoping she looked like one, too. She had donned Mr. Bleek's coat and tucked her long dark hair under his tricorne hat. With a patch over her eye and a gold earring, she looked like a convincing, if very small, pirate. Fortunately, Mr. Bleek was a short man himself. And she'd tucked a pillow under his coat to duplicate his well-fed stomach.

The only real problem had been his wooden leg. Before leaving the inn, she'd put on a pair of loose-fitting breeches she'd found in the laundry. That had been the easy part. She'd waited until she reached the beach, then bent her leg back as far as it would go. Around her leg she'd strapped a belt to keep it in place. The loose breeches nicely disguised her trick. Still, with the wooden leg on, she couldn't walk more than a few steps without falling.

"I hope this isn't a crazy idea," she whispered, but Bartholomew didn't answer. He hadn't said a word all the way here. She could have sworn he was trembling as much as she was.

A soft splashing noise met her ears. It was a moonless night, but Carmelita could just make out a small rowboat approaching from the north. In it were three men.

As they pulled the boat ashore and stalked toward her, Bartholomew took off, hightailing it for a cluster of trees. She couldn't blame him. She wanted to run, too. Unfortunately, she couldn't even walk.

"Ho!" one of the men called, his pistol pointed at Carmelita. "Bleek! Do that be you?"

Carmelita waved. She was afraid to speak. Her voice would surely give her away.

The three men came closer. They were dressed just like she was and smelled of rum and tobacco.

She could barely make out their faces in the gloom. One had a beard, and one was very tall.

"That ain't Bleek," one of the men whispered loudly.

They stopped short, pistols cocked. "Who goes there?" the bearded pirate demanded.

Carmelita held up the map. "It's me, Bleek, confound it," she muttered in her lowest, most pirate-sounding voice.

"If it's you," the man said, "what's got you all prissy-sounding?"

"I'm a bit under the weather, is all." Carmelita coughed. "Now take this blasted map, will you? I've got rum and a warm bed waitin'."

"Ain't Bleek," the tall pirate pronounced. "He ain't never gone to bed by midnight. And he looks too short by half."

Carmelita took a wobbly step backward. The wooden leg sank in the sand. Her heart hammered in her throat. There was no point in crying out. No one would hear her in this isolated inlet.

The men surrounded her, pistols at the ready. She was trapped!

"Tell us who you be, and tell us now," the bearded pirate barked.

"I . . . ," Carmelita coughed, "I—I—"

Suddenly, out of the dark sky, came a flutter of wings. Bartholomew! He landed right on Carmelita's shoulder.

Then he began to sing.

"Yo-ho, yo-ho, a pirate's life for me!"

"Well, shiver me soul!" the tall pirate cried. "It *is* Bleek! That's his loud-mouthed parrot, by thunder!"

"A pirate's life for me!" Bartholomew sang again.

"'Course it's me, you cussed fools," Carmelita muttered. "Now take that map and be off with you."

"Best be going," the bearded pirate said. "Cap'n'll be wantin' to study this map." He glanced back over his shoulder. "What's that? Did you hear anything? A howlin', like a ghost?"

The tall pirate winked at Carmelita. "Ol' Eagle Eye here swears we're bein' tracked by the ghost of Sharkheart Sam."

"He wants the viceroy's gold as fierce as we do," Eagle Eye said nervously. "And he's got more of a claim on it, truth to tell."

"Too bad he's sleepin' at the bottom of the sea!" the tall pirate said with a hearty laugh.

Carmelita watched them head off across the sand. A wave of relief washed over her.

"By the way," she called casually in a low voice, "when is that raid takin' place?"

"Tomorrow night, weather allowin'," answered Eagle Eye. He rubbed his hands together. "And there'll be plenty of gold and jewels for the takin'. Even for that mangy bird of yours, I reckon."As they climbed back into their boat, Carmelita stroked Bartholomew. "That's twice you've rescued me. I owe you. All of Zaragona will owe you, Bartholomew. I don't know how I'll ever repay you."

Bartholomew winked at her. "Gold and jewels," he replied. "Gold and jewels."

The pirates waved to Carmelita. She waved back. "Mangy birds," Bartholomew muttered.

"I couldn't agree with you more," Carmelita said with a laugh.

✕

The next day, the pirates of the *Sea Demon* tried to land. They crashed on the rocky coast, fooled by Carmelita's map.

Carmelita had managed to convince her parents

because Mr. Bleek was still groggy from his hit in the head and was willing to confess everything. Her parents had then gotten a message to the guards. The viceroy's men were waiting for the pirates, and they were all hauled to the city jails.

The following morning, Carmelita was cleaning Mr. Bleek's old room when she heard horses approaching. She looked out the window and saw a beautiful coach. Out stepped a handsome young man dressed in such finery that her breath stopped.

Carmelita dashed down the stairs with Bartholomew on her shoulder. Her mother and father were in the kitchen.

"Mama! Papa! Come quickly! The viceroy is here!" she shouted.

Her father winked. "Ah, not the viceroy again!"

Carmelita's mother patted her shoulder. "Our little heroine. Perhaps her head has grown too big, even for that hat of Mr. Bleek's!"

But just then the front door flew open. "His Excellency, the Viceroy of Zaragona," a guard announced.

Carmelita's mother gasped and curtsied. Her father bowed low. Carmelita curtsied, too.

But Bartholomew wasn't one for such pleasantries. He flew right over to the viceroy and perched on his shoulder.

"So this is the parrot who aided you in you daring

entrapment of the *Sea Demon?*" the viceroy asked.

"Gold and jewels, gold and jewels!" Bartholomew answered.

"I apologize, Your Excellency," Carmelita said quickly.

"Please. You may call me Pablo."

Carmelita smiled shyly. "Bartholomew's a pirate at heart, I'm afraid."

"I have a friend like him," Pablo said. "An orangutan, actually. She's getting a bit gray around the muzzle, but she's still a pirate to the bone." He snapped his finger and a guard passed him an iron chest. "As it happens, your friend, uh—"

"Bartholomew," Carmelita said.

"Bartholomew read my mind. I am here to reward you for saving Zaragona. In the name of the king, I present you with this token of our gratitude."

The guard opened the box. Carmelita gasped. It was filled to the brim with sparkling jewels!

"And I would be most grateful if you would take this ring as a token of my personal esteem," Pablo added. He removed his ruby ring and handed it to Carmelita.

"But . . . but I just did what anyone would have done."

"Quite the contrary," Pablo said. "You did what only the most extraordinary person would do."

Carmelita held the beautiful ring up to the light. In the blink of an eye, Bartholomew flapped over and grabbed the shiny jewel in his claws.

Carmelita just laughed. "He deserves it more than I do," she said as he sped out the open door, singing to himself.

She could just make out Bartholomew singing, "Yo-ho, yo-ho," as he headed off into the warm tropical winds.

SMILIN' JACK'S
LAST SMILE

After three days at sea on a makeshift raft, Josiah Smith knew he was seeing things. The great sloop gliding toward him had to be a mirage. He nudged Flash, his little black dog. "Am I crazy, Flash, or are we about to be saved?"

He waved frantically. His little raft nearly overturned. The slab of wood was all that remained of the *Adventure*, which had sunk in a terrible storm.

A lookout on the approaching ship returned Josiah's wave. "Is it an English ship, I wonder?" Josiah said excitedly. "No matter. As long as it floats, I'll be a willing passenger—"

He stopped short when he caught sight of the ship's flag. The skull and crossbones! Pirates! He was doomed.

As a rowboat from the sloop approached, Josiah

gathered his meager possessions together. He had nothing to offer the pirates, not a guinea to his name. The only things he'd managed to save were his paints and brushes—and, of course, Flash.

"He's no good to us," one of the pirates said as they neared Josiah's raft. "Let's shoot him now and be done with it."

"Captain said to bring him back, Zeke," another said. "I'm not one to argue with Smilin' Jack when his mood's as foul as that storm the other day."

Smilin' Jack! Josiah would have gulped, but his mouth was as dry as a desert. The crew of the *Adventure* had told Josiah many tales about the devilish pirate. He was as vain as they came, they'd said, always dressed like a king. And when he slit the throats of innocent men, he never stopped grinning.

Within minutes, Josiah was standing before Smilin' Jack himself. Sure enough, the pirate captain was dressed as if he were about to attend a palace ball—a yellow silk scarf around his neck, a blue silk sash around his large belly, a wide-brimmed black hat with dozens of colorful feathers on his head. He paused to admire his reflection in a bucket of water, carefully rearranging his black ringlets.

"I'm a good man, and a generous one," Jack said with a huge grin. "That's why I'm going to let you choose your fate. You can walk the plank. You can be hanged. Or you can be a thoughtful lad and just let me slit your throat right here and now."

"But . . . but I've done nothing wrong!" Josiah cried. "I was caught in the storm, on my way to the New World—"

"Quit your blasted begging" Jack interrupted. "You've got nothing. No gold. No jewels. You're of no use to me."

"But . . . but suppose I told you I could earn my keep?"

Jack laughed uproariously. "And how might that be?"

Josiah displayed his little leather case of paints and brushes. "I'm a portrait artist."

"You're a mere pup," Zeke exclaimed. "Artist indeed! Let's string him up by his thumbs from the yardarm, Cap'n!"

He grabbed for Josiah. Flash leapt to his master's defense with a fierce growl.

"Confounded cur!" Zeke screeched. "Why, I'll—"

"Silence, Zeke," Jack said. He turned to Josiah. "Are you saying that you could paint portrait of *me*?"

"As real as looking in a mirror."

"In my dancin' clothes?" Jack asked hopefully.

"Why, I could paint you on the king of England's throne, if you're willing."

"I've always wanted someone to capture me on canvas. The real me—kindhearted, generous of spirit, bold . . . We shall begin immediately. And if

I don't like your work, *then* I'll slit your throat."

"At least let me slice the mongrel's throat!" said Zeke.

"I . . . I can't paint without Flash," Josiah said quickly. "He's my inspiration. My muse."

"Cats mew, boy, not dogs," said Jack. "But I suppose you don't need to be a genius to put paint to paper." He shrugged. "Let the dog live. I had a dog once myself. Did fine tricks." He tossed a piece of wood across the deck. "Fetch, boy."

Flash promptly stood on his hind legs and twirled.

"No brighter than his master, I see. Well, I'm off to dress for my sitting." He gave Josiah a hearty pat on the back. "Boy, you're in for quite a treat. Two treats! The chance to paint me for posterity. And to join us in the greatest raid in the history of piracy! Our course is set for Zaragona!"

✕

For the next two weeks, as they sailed toward Zaragona, Smilin' Jack posed for Josiah every day. And every day, he decided Josiah had almost, but not quite, managed to capture his real self on paper.

Josiah painted Jack on the quarterdeck of the grandest frigate in the king's navy. He painted Jack riding a dolphin over the ocean waves. He painted Jack twenty years younger and a hundred pounds lighter. But nothing was ever quite right.

Since he had no canvas, Josiah painted over a landscape painting, part of the booty Smilin' Jack's crew had captured from a Spanish galleon. Once one painting had dried, Josiah painted another right over it.

Jack was posing on the quarterdeck for Josiah one afternoon when the winds picked up. The sails filled as if they would burst. The ship rode the waves, bucking wildly.

"I fear a big storm's brewin', Cap'n," reported Snake, one of the pirate lieutenants. "Could even be a hurricane. It's early yet, but the crew can smell it in the wind."

"Maintain your course!" Jack ordered, careful not to change his pose. "We're just a day out of Zaragona."

"Cap'n." Snake lowered his voice. "Last night, two men on watch swore they caught sight of the ghost ship."

"Ghost ship?" Josiah asked.

"Sharkheart Sam's ship. He's roamin' the seas, just waitin' for the day when he can locate all of his treasure."

"Foolish superstition. Besides, the ghost of Sharkheart can forget it," Smilin' Jack declared. "That treasure is nothing compared to what will be ours before long!"

"There's plenty of other treasure in places easier to take than Zaragona," Snake pointed out.

"Perhaps if we changed course—"

"Spineless lubber," Jack sneered. "Marito is a strategic port. If we capture it, we rule all the Caribbean!"

"As you wish, sir," Snake muttered. As he turned to leave, he tripped over Flash. "Cussed cur," he said.

Flash gave a menacing growl. "Sit, Flash," Josiah ordered.

Flash considered, they lay down and rolled over.

"I've seen fish with more brains," said Snake.

Josiah stroked Flash's ear. "He's just independent." Josiah gazed out at the cloudy horizon. Another day, and they'd be landing in Zaragona. He knew the pirates expected him to join in the raid.

Somehow, someway, he had to find a way to escape.

✕

By the next evening, the storm had picked up force. The ship raced along the rocky coast. The winds screamed fiercely. Rain lashed the deck.

Josiah stood on the quarterdeck with Smilin' Jack, Snake, and Zeke. "If we ain't careful, Cap'n," Snake said, "those rocks'll be our graveyard yet."

"Steady as she goes," Jack said. His soaked hat sagged around his curls, its feathers drooping. "I can almost taste that gold, boys."

They passed a dark expanse of rock. The mouth

of a large cave was visible in the flashes of lightning that sliced the sky. Suddenly an earsplitting howl came from the mouth of the cave. It sounded like a great beast in terrible pain.

Snake and Zeke fell to the deck. All over the ship, pirates cried out in terror and dashed for cover. "It's the ghost of Sharkheart Sam, warnin' us off!" Snake cried.

"It's the wind, you fools!" Jack shouted. "Besides, we've real dangers ahead. There lies the fortress of Marito! No ghosts, but real men with real cannons!"

As if to prove Jack's point, a huge boom filled the air, louder than any thunder. The cannonball fired from the fort landed short, about a hundred yards off the starboard bow.

Instantly the crew came alive, dashing about madly on the dark, slick decks. "Charge your cannons, me hearties!" Jack ordered. "These are the viceroy's men firing on us, not ghosts! Fire when ready!"

The noise was deafening. Flash crawled under a tarp and covered his ears with his paws. Josiah felt like hiding, too. But there was something mesmerizing about the great red-orange blasts of light and the wild booms shaking the very decks.

Straight into the cannon barrage the ship headed. "Let's give her a broadside, men!" Jack cried.

All the cannons fired in unison. Suddenly the cannons of the fort fell silent. "Direct hit!" Zeke

yelled, and the other pirates cheered.

"No time for patting ourselves on the back," the captain said. "Men, drop anchor and prepare to go ashore!"

Within minutes, Josiah found himself crowded into a longboat with Jack and members of his crew. Other boats followed close behind. Flash sat at Josiah's feet, nosing the wind. The rain fell in torrents. Waves crashed over the side. Musket shots from the soldiers onshore whizzed past the pirates' heads. Josiah and the others crouched low, but Smilin' Jack sat tall in the bow, grinning with delight.

"*Buzzard*'s Bounty is the richest fortune the Caribbean's ever seen," Jack said. "There's a strong-box Sharkheart used to keep in his pillow. Full of rubies and diamonds the size of hen's eggs, they say, and if that weren't enough we've got all the king's gold as well."

Just then, a shot rang out. It tore right through Jack's favorite hat. He put a finger through the front hole, glowering. "You'll pay for this, you miserable dogs!" he shouted at the fort.

Pistols blazing, the longboats landed right at the town dock. Josiah whistled for Flash. Dodging musketballs, they ran with the pirates a short distance. When they passed a dark alley, Josiah slipped into it.

"We'll be safe here, Flash," he said breathlessly. "I'll wager they'll have Jack and the boys locked up before long. Jack's wily, but he's no match for the viceroy's men. At least, I hope not."

For well over an hour, Josiah and Flash hid in the alley while the battle raged. At last Josiah couldn't stand waiting any longer. What if Jack and his men really took over Marito? Josiah had to know what was happening.

Josiah slipped up and down the alleys. Some of Smilin' Jack's crew seemed to have decided they'd already won the battle.

Turning a corner, Josiah was surprised to see one of Jack's lieutenants wallowing in the mud, singing happily to himself. A jug of rum was nearby. Several curious pigs surrounded him, snorting and sniffing.

Suddenly a woman burst out of the upper floor of a house, broom in hand. She was chasing another pirate. He was running as if his life depended on it.

In the town square, Josiah found Smilin' Jack with Zeke and Snake, all standing around a well. Zeke had a guitar. Snake had an accordion. They were serenading themselves with a jaunty sea chantey. A donkey and dog sat nearby, listening attentively. "Yo-ho, yo-ho, a pirate's life for me," the men sang.

To Josiah's horror, he realized that the pirates were dangling a helpless man inside the well! He was dressed like an important person. The pirates lowered him into the water, then raised him up again.

Each time the pirates yanked him up he begged for mercy as he gasped for air.

"This is pirate mercy," Zeke sneered. "We ain't killed you yet, have we?"

Josiah watched in horror as they lowered the man again. "Let's leave him down a little longer, boys," Jack suggested. "See how long he can hold his breath."

Josiah could stand it no longer. He leapt from the barrel with Flash at his heels.

"Well, if it ain't the painter boy," Zeke said, "and his mangy mongrel."

Just then, Flash caught sight of a rat and raced off in pursuit.

"Flash!" Josiah called. "Come, boy!" But as usual, Flash would not obey. He glanced back at Josiah, stood on his hind legs and barked, then ran off.

"Dumbest dog in all history," Snake said, spitting.

"Where you been?" Smilin' Jack asked. "You're missing the party! We're having ourselves a little drowning."

"I . . . uh, got sidetracked." Josiah glanced at the well. The man had been under a very long time. Josiah had to do something, and quick.

"Captain," Josiah said quickly, "down the street, I saw a tavern with more ale than a hundred crews could drink. And not a soul in sight! There was fresh smoked pig and fruit in all the colors of the rainbow. I'd have liked to paint it. A fine still life, it would have made."

The captain peered down the well. "This here's a still life already, in my opinion. Be a stiff life, soon enough. Har har! Come on, men! Down the street you say, lad?"

"Three blocks, sir, starboard side of the street. I'll be along to join you as soon as I find Flash."

When the pirates were out of sight, Josiah cranked the well handle. Each turn was a struggle. But after three false attempts, the man's head popped above water.

"Sir?" Josiah called down the well. "You all right?"

"I've been better," the man sputtered. His eyes went wide. "Oh . . . but you're one of the pirates!"

"No, sir," Josiah said. "I'm Josiah Smith. I was a prisoner of Smilin' Jack. I aim to save you, if I can."

Pulling as hard as he could, Josiah managed to get the man to the top of the well. "Here, take my hand."

"Boy, when we've vanquished these buccaneers, I'll see to it you're handsomely rewarded," the man said. "I am the mayor of this town, and the viceroy is my grandfather."

"First things first," Josiah said. "Your hand."

Josiah yanked, bracing his foot against the stone well. "Push off the side of the well with your feet," he instructed. "One, two, three—"

Suddenly the mayor tumbled out of the well, plowing into Josiah. They skidded across the ground, right into a stone statue of the viceroy.

"Well, at least you're out," Josiah said, but the mayor didn't answer. "Sir?"

The mayor had been knocked out cold! Josiah shook him hard. "Sir? Wake up!"

"Unhand the mayor, scoundrel!" someone called.

The viceroy's soldiers! So the pirates hadn't won yet. Josiah sighed with relief. "Actually," he said, "I saved his life. You see—"

"That'll be the day, when one of Smilin' Jack's boys saves the viceroy's only grandson!"

"But I swear I was a prisoner—"

"And so you shall be one again," the guard said. He yanked Josiah to his feet and marched him to the jail.

✕

"Well, look who's here. If it ain't the traitor himself."

As Josiah was tossed into the cold, damp prison, he was shocked to see Smilin' Jack and Zeke, sitting glumly in the corner on the dirt floor.

The gate closed behind him with a clang. "Enjoy the company while you can," said the guard. "You'll be hanged at dawn."

Josiah gazed out between the cold metal bars. Well, at least Flash was still free. Perhaps he'd be all right. He was a tough old dog. He'd find a new master. The thought made tears spring to Josiah's eyes. He turned to the pirates. "What happened to you?" he asked.

"We was set up, that's what," Zeke declared. "That tavern you sent us to was crawling with the viceroy's men. Snake got away, but we was caught. Outnumbered, we was, a hundred to one."

"I ought to wring your scrawny neck," Smilin' Jack added with a nasty grin. "Never did like your paintings. Not a one captured my inner beauty."

Josiah sat in the dirt on the other side of the jail. After a few minutes, Smilin' Jack and Snake fell asleep, snoring loudly. The guard stationed outside their cell was asleep, too. He had a musket cradled in his arms. Josiah could see the silver ring of keys in his pocket. He tried to reach his arm through the bars and grab them, but the keys were just out of reach.

When he was about to give up, he heard a familiar soft bark.

"Flash?" he whispered. "Is that you, boy?"

There was Flash, proudly displaying a rat he'd caught.

"Flash," Josiah whispered. "I need your help. This is our only chance, boy, so you've got to get it right. See those keys?" Josiah pointed through the bars to the key ring. "Fetch them, boy! Fetch them for me!"

Flash cocked his head to one side, considering.

"That's right, boy, fetch the keys!" Josiah whispered. He crossed his fingers. *For once, Flash*, he silently prayed, *get it right*.

With a confident swagger, Flash headed to the guard. He sniffed him over for good measure, then nudged the keys.

"Gently, boy. There's a good dog," Josiah said. "Bring 'em here, boy! Fetch!"

Flash hesitated. Suddenly his eyes brightened. He wagged his tail furiously.

He leaped onto his hind legs and spun in wild circles, barking uproariously.

Josiah covered his eyes and groaned. The guard woke with a start. So did the pirates.

"It's that confounded cur again!" Zeke cried.

"I said *fetch*, boy," Josiah moaned.

Flash stopped his trick. He looked very disappointed.

The guard climbed to his feet unsteadily. He aimed his musket at Flash.

"No!" Josiah cried. "Run, Flash, run!"

Flash considered. After a second, he lay on his back and rolled—right into the feet of the guard.

"Whoa!" The guard tripped and staggered. He landed hard on the ground.

BOOM! The guard's musket fired into the air. The key ring rolled out of his pocket. The guard, terrified by the sound of his own gun, yelled, "Don't kill me! Don't kill me!"

Josiah snatched up the keys. In an instant, he opened the door. He slid out and slammed the bars back in Smilin' Jack's face.

"Let me out of here, you ungrateful whelp!" Smilin' Jack yelled.

But Josiah was busy. He yanked the guard's cutlass

from his belt and held it to the man's throat. "Take me to the viceroy now," Josiah commanded.

"But Josiah, boy," Smilin' Jack pleaded. "I'm your pal, your best friend. You can't leave me here!"

"My best friend," Josiah said with a laugh, "has four legs, Captain, and he can't follow an order to save his life."

Flash grabbed his dead rat and wagged his tail jubilantly. With the guard in the lead, Josiah and Flash headed off to the viceroy's mansion.

When he glanced back at Jack one last time, Josiah was surprised. It was the first time he'd ever seen Jack without his famous smile.

X

By the next morning, all of Smilin' Jack's crew had been captured. The mayor had recovered and explained how Jack had rescued him. Josiah was welcomed into the viceroy's mansion, where he was treated as a hero. He slept on a feather bed, dined on fresh oranges, and regaled the viceroy and his wife, a regal woman named Carmelita, with tales of his life on Smilin' Jack's ship.

As soon as the storm had passed, the viceroy arranged for passage to the continent of the New World for Josiah and Flash. As Josiah prepared to board the ship, Carmelita took him aside. "I know of a little girl who saved this beautiful paradise once before. She, too, received a reward, and now she wants to pass it on to you."

Josiah bowed gratefully. "I've no need of it. I am an artist, not a pirate. From what I've seen, riches only bring trouble. They were certainly Smilin' Jack's downfall. As long as I have my paints and Flash, I'll be happy."

"Well, that is perfect then," said Carmelita. "For that is just what I have brought you. Fresh paints and brushes." She handed him a small iron chest.

As the ship left port, Josiah opened his new paints. Amazing! Every color he could ever want, and new brushes, too!

He lifted the tin of paints. To his surprise, there was something under them.

Something glittering.

Josiah shook his head. Rubies, diamonds, emeralds, the size of his fist! Too many to count, a fortune beyond imagining.

"Flash," Josiah said, holding up a ruby to the light, "it seems we are going to be wealthy men, after all, whether we like it or not."

Just then the ship pitched to the right. Josiah lost his grip on the ruby. It skittered across the deck.

"Fetch, boy," Josiah said.

Flash cocked his head, considering.

Josiah tried again. "Fetch."

With a gleam in his eye, Flash rolled onto the deck and played dead.

"Good boy," Josiah said with a laugh. One thing was certain. Riches would never change old Flash.

He'd always been an independent sort of fellow.

THE SECRET
TREASURE MAP

Alicia Smith urged her Arabian horse, Turbo, into an all-out gallop. They flew across the Louisiana countryside in a furious tornado of energy.

And Alicia was angry, so angry that tears streamed down her face. Her father had just delivered the news she'd feared—they could no longer keep Turbo. A recent hurricane had destroyed all of the Smiths' crops, and they were going to have to sell the farm.

And without the farm, there would be no way to keep Turbo.

In one tremendous bound, Turbo sailed over the wooden fence that separated the Smiths' land from the highway. She slowed him to an easy trot and headed in the direction of her best friend, Mike Bateman, who lived about half a mile away. She didn't have to show Turbo the way. He knew it by heart.

How many days had they ridden over to Mike's? And for how many years? Alicia and Mike had been friends since the day she'd forced him to eat a mud pie in nursery school. (He'd somehow found it in his heart to forgive her.)

Mike's family had also been devastated by the wrath of Hurricane Sam. His father's office had been demolished, and part of the roof had been torn off Mike's home. After realizing it would cost too much to rebuild, the family had decided to move out of state. They were leaving in a few days.

It was too much to bear. Because of the hurricane, Alicia was going to lose her two best friends in the world—Mike *and* Turbo.

Alicia tied Turbo to the fence outside Mike's house. The white picket fence was one of the few things in the neighborhood left untouched by Hurricane Sam.

Mike was already waiting for her, armed with a carrot and apple slices for Turbo. He gave the shiny black stallion a carrot, while Alicia buried her face in Turbo's silky mane.

"How are you holding up?" Mike asked gently.

"It's just so unfair," Alicia cried. "To lose you and Turbo . . . all at once."

"As soon as you called me, I started trying to think

of some way for you to keep Turbo," Mike said.

"And keep you from moving, too?" Alicia said. "Not likely."

"We could rob a bank," Mike suggested lamely.

"On Turbo," Alicia said. "Jesse and Jenny James. Somehow I can't see it. Besides, half the banks in town were destroyed by the hurricane."

"Maybe we'll come into a fortune. Don't you have any long-lost relatives who put you in their will?"

Alicia wiped her eyes. "Just good ol' Josiah Smith. But I wouldn't count on him, if you know what I mean."

They laughed ruefully. Alicia's grandfather, who lived nearby, had regaled them for years with stories about Josiah. According to Gramps, as he was known to just about everyone, Josiah had died a very wealthy man. He'd left behind a fortune in treasure, so the story went. Unfortunately, nobody knew just where.

The truth was, no one took Gramps's stories *too* seriously. He also believed that the family was related to both Queen Elizabeth and David Letterman. And he swore to anyone who'd listen that he'd been abducted by an alien who wanted his chili recipe.

"This is one time I wish Gramps was right," Alicia said with a weary smile. "Which reminds me. I promised I'd help him clean up his yard this afternoon. You up for it?"

"Sure. He's more entertaining than my family. Everybody's moping about the move."

"Join the club." With a sigh, Alicia mounted Turbo. Mike joined her, and together they rode the short distance to her grandfather's house.

Gramps was in his garage—or what remained of it. The hurricane had spared most of his house, but the garage had lost one wall. Unfortunately, the garage was where Gramps had stored all his precious junk—and he had a lot of it. Every weekend he went to garage sales, and he never left one without buying something. A set of bongos. A two-spouted teapot. An autographed photo of Lassie. (Alicia always wondered how a dog could manage to autograph a picture.) It didn't matter, as long as Gramps bought something.

Now all his junk was distributed around the yard and far beyond. A stuffed elephant hung from the branch of an oak tree. A pair of red long johns draped the mailbox across the street.

"Wow," Alicia said as she hopped off Turbo. "Looks like we have our work cut out for us."

"I'm so sorry about Turbo," Alicia's grandfather said, hugging her close. "You kids are having a bad spin of luck, that's for sure. Tell you what. I'll go whip up some of my special extra chocolatey hot chocolate."

"Gramps," Alicia said gently, "it's eighty-five degrees out."

He winked. "That's what makes it so special. It's

unexpected. And the unexpected is what makes life interesting."

"Hurricane Sam was unexpected," Mike pointed out grimly.

"That was quite a wind we had," Gramps said. I've seen hurricanes come and seen 'em go, but Sam was a mean bugger. It's amazing no one was seriously hurt."

Mike grabbed a large trash bag. "So where do we start?"

The old man rubbed his chin. "Thought maybe I'd make a fresh start of it. Throw everything away, build a new garage, start my collection from scratch."

"Should we save anything?" Alicia asked.

"Hmm. There's a Statue of Liberty ashtray I picked up recently. And oh, the stuffed chipmunk lamp. That's a collector's item. And that oil painting over there by the paint cans, I've always been fond of that."

Alicia tried not to smile at the painting of a grinning pirate. "Which garage sale did that come from, Gramps?"

"Oh, that's been in the family for years," he replied. "It's a Josiah Smith original. Your grandmother won't let me bring it in the house. Says it's tacky." He shrugged. "No accounting for taste, I suppose."

Mike and Alicia got down to work, sorting and

tossing. Inside a toolbox filled with odds and ends, Mike found a black eye patch. He tried it on for Alicia. "*Aargh!*" he cried. "Shiver me timbers, matey!"

Alicia gave him a halfhearted smile.

"What? Don't I make it as a pirate?"

Gramps returned to the garage holding a tray of steaming mugs of hot chocolate. "I think you make a fine pirate, Mike," he said. "You know, that fortune of Josiah's was rumored to have come from pirate treasure."

"Pirates!" Alicia rolled her eyes. "Pirates are just in movies and amusement park rides."

"Ah, but there's where you're wrong. Josiah's treasure, an iron box of priceless gems, first belonged to a dastardly pirate named Sharkheart Sam. A young boy by the name of Pablo—a bit of a pickpocket, so the story goes—stole them from ol' Sharkheart. Pablo went on to become the viceroy of Zaragona, and he gave the treasure to a brave girl named Carmelita, who later became his wife." He smiled. "And that's where ol' Josiah came into the picture. Carmelita passed the treasure on to him, buy he was a miserly old guy, Josiah. Made what money he needed painting portraits. Never spent a penny of his fortune. My great-great-grandpa swore *his* grandpa swore Josiah buried it in a cave."

"Well, it's a nice story anyway," Alicia said with a fond smile. "Hey, what should I do with those paint cans?"

"Just stack 'em up, hon. Never know when I might want to paint the house again." Last round, he'd opted for a brilliant shade of violet. Alicia's grandmother had nearly fainted when she saw it.

"Well, I'm off for a little nap," Gramps said. "You kids keep anything you like, hear? And thanks again."

"I'm sure going to miss his stories," Mike said when Gramps was gone.

Alicia felt hot tears sting her eyes. She set the ugly pirate painting against the wall, then busied herself rearranging the stacks of paint cans and thinner and the piles or brushes that her grandfather had collected over the past year.

"We're running out of garbage bags," Mike announced. "This may set a new record."

"There are some on that tool shelf, if I can reach them," Alicia said. On tiptoe, she was just able to touch the box of bags. As she pulled it down, she lost her balance. She fell backward into the cans of paint and thinner and sent them crashing. A glass jar filled with paint thinner splashed onto the wall and floor.

"Are you okay?" Mike asked, rushing over.

"Yeah, but man, what a mess," Alicia moaned.

"Man, what a stink," Mike added as the sharp smell of the thinner filled the air. Don't worry about the mess, though. This place was already a disaster area!"

"Toss me those paper towels," Alicia said. Suddenly she gasped. "Uh-oh."

"Uh-oh what?"

"The thinner. It splashed all over that hideous pirate painting! Quick! The towels!"

Frantically, Alicia wiped off the painting. But all she managed to do was make a smeary mess.

"The paint's coming off!" she cried. "Gramps really liked this painting, too."

"Actually, I think you've improved it," Mike joked.

Alicia kept wiping gently, hoping against hope she could salvage the painting.

"Hey, Alicia?" Mike said as he stared over her

shoulder. "I know this sounds crazy, but there's something under that pirate."

Alicia paused "It's some kind of map, I think. Look, there. Sweetwater Pond! That's near us!"

Mike grabbed a paper towel and began to work on another corner. "And here! Near the spring, there's a cave!"

"That's the Bat Cave," Alicia said. "I'll bet you anything." The Bat Cave, as it was known, was familiar to everyone in the area. The home to hundreds of bats, it was rumored to be haunted. No one ventured near it.

Mike pointed to a black **X** near the cave. "Alicia, are you thinking what I'm thinking?"

"That Gramps is going to kill me?"

"That he's going to thank his lucky stars you're such a klutz!"

"I am not—"

"Alicia, this is a treasure map!" Miked scrubbed at another spot, revealing old-fashioned writing. "'Treasure here, twelve paces north-northeast from one-armed oak into cave,' " Mike read. " 'Under the Flash.' "

He stared at Alicia. Alicia stared back. "Treasure?" they said in unison.

"We are outta here," Mike said. "Let's see, we'll need a flashlight, a shovel—"

"Mike," Alicia said firmly, "it'll be dark soon, and that cave is full of bats. Not to mention that it's totally haunted."

"Bats don't scare me."

"Yeah, well ghosts scare me."

Mike grabbed her by the shoulders. "Do you know what a treasure could mean? Do you know what it could mean to you and me?"

Just then, as if in answer, Turbo let out a plaintive neigh.

"You get the light," Alicia said. "I'll get the shovel."

✕

By the time they neared the cave, it was dark. A sliver of moon and Mike's flashlight provided their only light.

"Alicia, I'm starting to have second thoughts," Mike said as they approached the Bat Cave. Behind

them, Turbo shuffled nervously at the tree where they'd tied him. "I mean, they call this the Bat Cave for a reason. And one-armed oak? What's that about?"

Alicia shone the flashlight on the map they'd copied onto a piece of paper. "Okay, so maybe it's insane. But what do we have to lose?"

"Well, first we need to figure out what the heck a one-armed oak is," Mike pointed out.

Alicia aimed the flashlight at tree after tree. "There!" Mike cried. "See that tree?"

Sure enough, a large oak stood before them. A huge branch extended out on one side like a gnarled arm.

"Okay, then," Alicia said, fighting the fear that gripped at her. "Twelve paces north-northeast into the cave."

Mike pulled a compass out of his pocket. "I wasn't a Boy Scout for nothing," he said. "Okay. Here goes."

Together, following the lead of the compass, they carefully began to pace their way inside the cave. At the mouth, they both hesitated. "How do we know what a pace is?" Alicia asked. "Josiah probably took bigger steps than we do. Maybe we should try again."

"We don't even know if this *is* a treasure map," Mike replied. "For all we know, it's an elaborate practical joke. Let's just get it over with. Ready?"

"Ready as I'll ever be," Alicia replied.

Mike's flashlight barely pierced the gloom inside the cave. Overhead, the noise of bats fluttering back and forth filled the air with an eerie whir.

"Two more paces," Mike said. They stopped. "Now the map says 'Under the Flash.' I wonder what that could mean?"

"There's no flash in here except the one coming from your light," Alicia said. "It's pitch-black—"

Her words were interrupted by a low, eerie howl.

"Mike?" she whispered. "That wasn't a—a—"

"Ghostly howl from the undead?" Mike gulped. "Nope. I'm pretty sure a ghostly howl from the undead would be more convincing. It's . . . It's probably just the wind. Probably."

Alicia took a step toward the door. "Look, we did what the map said. There's no flash. This is probably all some hoax. How about we try again tomorrow? In the daylight."

"Maybe that's what Josiah meant. Maybe you have to be here in the day, and there's some trick of the light—"

Suddenly something brushed against Alicia's face. "Gross! A bat touched me! I'm getting out of here!"

She started for the entrance, but her foot caught on a rock and she fell with a grunt. "Klutz strikes again," she muttered.

Mike rushed back to help her. "Come on! I have a creepy feeling the bats don't want us here. One just brushed by me, too. And if they don't want me here, I'll be glad to leave!"

But Alicia was busy examining the rock she'd tripped over. "Hand me your flashlight," she said. She pointed to a small painting on top of the rock. "It's a little black dog!"

"Very nice. Although I think the proportions are a little off. Can we please go now?"

"Mike, why would someone paint a picture of a dog in the middle of a cave full of bats? Suppose 'Flash' is a *name*, not a *thing*?"

She yanked at the rock. It would not give way. Another bat ruffled her hair as it swooped past.

"Well, I suppose it's worth a try," Mike said. Together they both pulled at the stubborn rock.

The howling increased. Nervously, Mike and Alicia tugged harder. The rock moved a little. Another yank. Another.

Suddenly the rock gave way. Underneath is was a dusty iron box. "Whoa," Alicia whispered.

"Whoa? Is that a *good* whoa?"

"It could be, like, the most major whoa of our lives," Alicia confirmed.

With trembling hands, she pried open the box. She gasped. Mike gasped.

Rubies! Emeralds! Diamonds! They glittered in the light from the flashlight.

The box was filled to the brim with every jewel imaginable.

"It was all true!" Alicia said in awe, donning a diamond necklace. "Gramps was right! There was a treasure!"

"Alicia," Mike said laughing. "Do you know what this means?"

"It means we can keep the farm and I can keep Turbo and you can stay here!"

"That's not all," Mike said. "If Gramps was right about this, it means he could be right about all kinds of things. It means, Alicia, that somewhere out there, an alien may actually be enjoying some of your grandfather's killer chili."